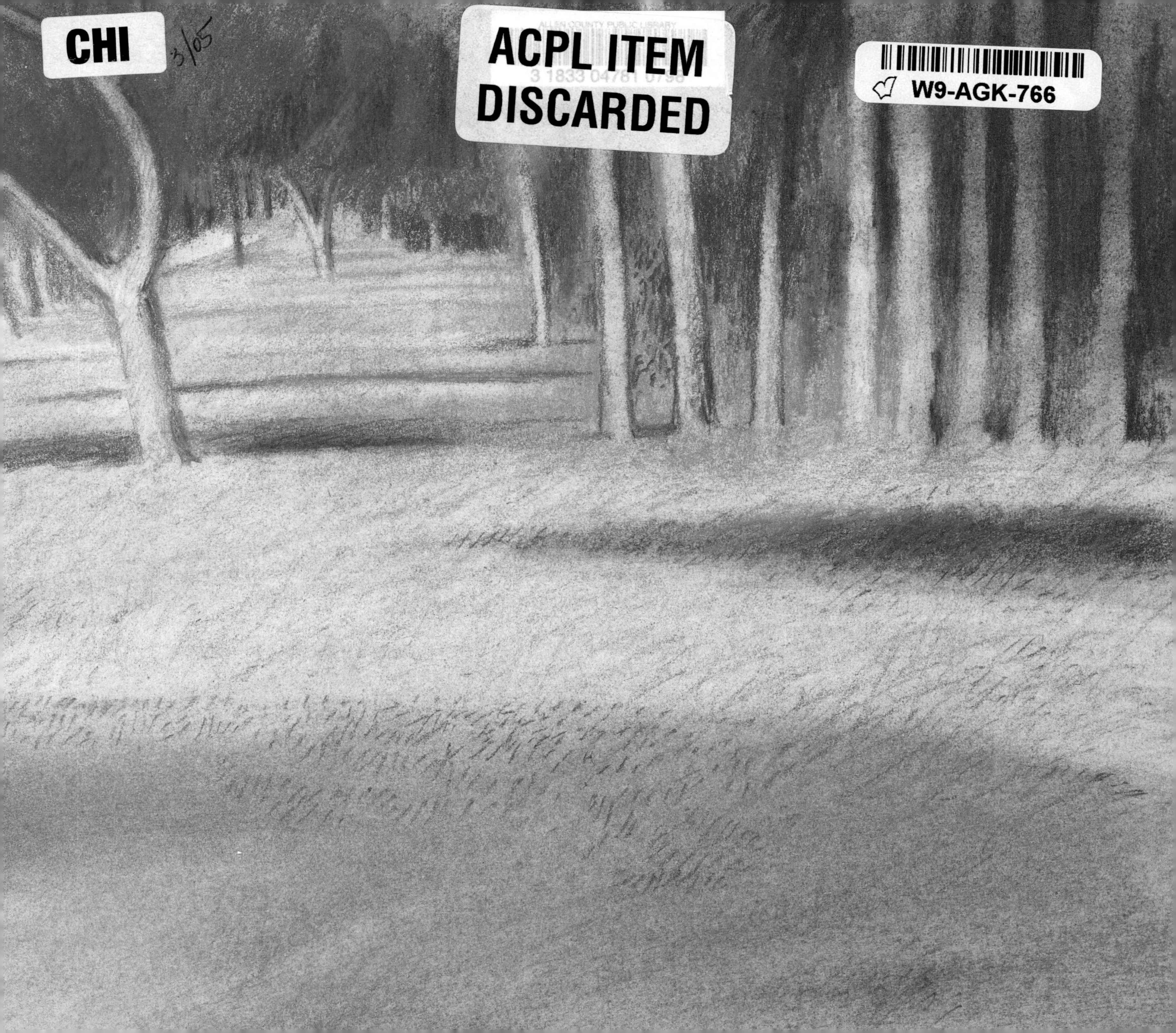

Katie's Sunday Afternoon

JAMES MAYHEW

ORCHARD BOOKS/NEW YORK

An Imprint of Scholastic Inc.

For little Katie Light

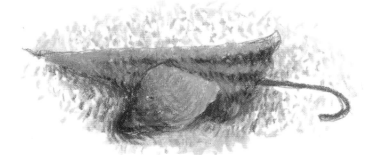

*and for Vanessa Hadfield
and Liz Johnson
(I couldn't have done it without you!)*

Library of Congress Cataloging-in-Publication Data available
ISBN 0-439-60678-0
10 9 8 7 6 5 4 3 2 1   05 06 07 08
Printed in Belgium
First Scholastic edition, March 2005
Reinforced Binding for Library Use

It was a sunny day, and Katie and Grandma were feeling very hot.

"Let's go swimming," said Grandma. "I'll get our swimsuits."

When they got to the pool, it was already full.

"Never mind, we'll come back later," said Grandma. "The art gallery is nearby. Let's go there for a while."

In the gallery, it felt even hotter! While Grandma had a little snooze, Katie found a room full of amazing pictures. They were painted in thousands of brightly colored dots.

Katie saw a painting called *Bathers at Asnières* by Georges Seurat.
She could almost feel the breeze blowing over the soft grass and
hear the gurgling river. "What a great place for a swim!" thought
Katie, so she climbed over the frame and inside the picture.

It was warm and peaceful in the picture—the sun
shone, oars splashed, and a boy in a red hat called to
the boats racing on the river. Katie saw a little bathing
hut and decided to change into her swimsuit . . .

. . . then Katie jumped into the water with an enormous *splash*!

"*Bonjour!*" said the boy in the red hat. "I'm Jacques."

"I'm Katie," she said. "Isn't this lovely?"

"*Oui!*" laughed Jacques. "*Très bon!*"

After lots more splashing, Katie
sat down on the picture frame to
rest. But it started to tip . . .

. . . and the river began pouring into the gallery!

"This is better than the swimming pool!" Katie laughed.

But then they heard a sigh from another painting by Seurat called *Sunday Afternoon on the Island of La Grande Jatte*. Katie saw a little girl in a white dress. She looked rather sad, so Katie climbed inside the picture.

Katie found herself in a park where everyone looked very elegant and grand.

"Oh, you are lucky," sighed the little girl. "It's such a hot day but no one is allowed to swim in this painting."

"Come and wade in the gallery!" said Katie. "It's lovely and cool."

"Oh Prudence, please say yes!" pleaded the girl to her governess.

"Well, be sure to keep your clothes dry, Josette," said Prudence.

"What a splendid idea!" said the elegant people. "Let's wade, too!"
The ladies hitched up their skirts and the gentlemen rolled up their trousers, and they all had a wonderful time wading in the gallery.

But water was still pouring out of the painting . . .

"It's getting too deep to wade," said Josette, standing on the steps.

"How will we get back to our picture?" said the elegant people. "We can't swim in these clothes!"

"Let's fetch a boat!" said Katie. She pointed to another picture
by Seurat called *Port of Honfleur*. Katie and Jacques swam over
to the painting and quickly clambered inside.

They found a little rowboat in the harbor.
It was quite heavy but they managed to drag
it over the frame and into the gallery. Then off
they rowed to the rescue!

"We'll go first!" said Prudence,
helping Josette into the boat.
  But when it was her turn,
  her foot slipped,
  the boat moved away and . . .

Splash!

Prudence fell into the water!
"Just look at my dress!" she
wailed. "How will I ever get dry?"

"Perhaps she'll help," said Katie, pointing to a picture called *Woman Hanging up the Washing* by Camille Pissarro. Prudence scrambled inside the picture, followed by Katie and Josette. Meanwhile, Jacques rowed off to rescue the elegant people and take them back to their picture.

The kindly washerwoman gave Prudence some clothes to wear and hung out her wet dress to dry. Then Katie, Josette, and the washerwoman's daughter played in the sun as the women chatted.

Suddenly, Katie heard Jacques calling from the boat.

"We must get back to our pictures," said Jacques. "The guard is coming!"

"The guard!" gasped Katie. "He'll be horrified when he sees all this water!"

"Quickly! Jump aboard!" called Jacques.

Prudence changed back into her clothes and carefully stepped into the boat. Katie and Josette leaped in after her.

Jacques rowed across the gallery while Katie desperately tried to think of a way to get rid of the water. They passed all sorts of pictures; none of them looked very useful. Then Katie saw a picture by Paul Signac called *Portrait of Felix Feneon*.

"He looks like a magician," said Katie. So she yelled, "Excuse me, can you do any magic? The gallery is a mess and the guard is coming!"

Felix wanted to help, so he leaned out of the painting, waved his stick over his hat, and shouted, "Abracadabra!"

Colored swirls came out of his picture, but the gallery was still flooded.

"I'll try again," he said. "Alla-kazam!"

"Oh dear," said Felix, as stars and rainbows floated into the gallery. "I'm not very good at magic."

Just then, they all heard footsteps. It was the guard!
"Oh, please try once more!" begged Katie.
"Alla-kazoom! Clear up this room!" said Felix.

There was a flash of light and everything
vanished in a swirl of stars and colors.

Katie found she was standing in her dry
clothes and everyone and everything was
back where it belonged—just in time!

The guard looked carefully around the
room. Everything was exactly as it should be.
"Thank you everyone," whispered Katie.
"I've had a wonderful time!"

As soon as the guard had gone, Katie gently woke Grandma.

"Would you like to go swimming now?" yawned Grandma.

"I don't feel quite so hot anymore!" laughed Katie.

"In that case, you won't be wanting an ice cream either,"
said Grandma.

"Oh, I can always manage an ice cream," said Katie.

"Me too!" smiled Grandma. And off they went.

More about the Pointillists

The painters Seurat, Signac, and Pissarro were called Pointillists. The Pointillists liked to keep their colors pure, so they didn't mix them together before they applied them to the canvas. They painted their pictures entirely in dots, deliberately placing contrasting or complementary colors next to one another to create different effects. This painting style not only kept colors vivid but seemed to capture both the scene and its atmosphere. At the time, many people didn't like Pointillist paintings—perhaps they found them fuzzy or messy—but painting in the Pointillist style took a long time and required a great deal of patience! Today, Pointillism is loved by many.

GEORGES SEURAT (1859-91)

Georges Seurat was the first artist to develop the Pointillist style of painting. If you look closely at his paintings you can see they are made up of brightly colored dots, but from a distance the colored dots seem to blend together, creating new shades. In this way, Seurat could keep his colors bright, making the pictures rich and lively. *Bathers at Asnières* is an early example of this, and you can see it at the National Gallery in London.

Seurat is particularly famous for his paintings of vacation spots, such as *Sunday Afternoon on the Island of La Grande Jatte*, which you can see at the Art Institute of Chicago, or *Port of Honfleur*, which can be seen at The Barnes Foundation in Merion, Pennsylvania.

PAUL SIGNAC (1863-1935)

Paul Signac was a great admirer of Seurat's paintings. Signac also painted in the Pointillist style, but in his later pictures, he applied the paint in mosaic-like squares, instead of dots. *Portrait of Felix Feneon*, shows Signac's friend, an important French art critic, against a backdrop of swirling patterns which seems to capture his lively personality. You can see *Portrait of Felix Feneon* at The Museum of Modern Art in New York City.

CAMILLE PISSARRO (1830-1903)

Camille Pissarro was born in the West Indies but later came to Paris to study art. Camille loved to explore France and painted the scenes he saw right on the spot, in the open air. He also admired Seurat's ideas and painted in the Pointillist style for several years. His pictures have large brush strokes, blurring into each other, creating a soft, dreamy look. A good example is *Woman Hanging up the Washing*, which you can see at the Musée d'Orsay in Paris, France.

ACKNOWLEDGEMENTS

Bathers at Asnières (1884) by Georges Seurat, National Gallery, London, UK/Bridgeman Art Library. *Sunday Afternoon on the Island of La Grande Jatte* (1884-86) by Georges Seurat, Art Institute of Chicago, IL, USA/Bridgeman Art Library. *Port of Honfleur* (c.1886) by Georges Seurat, The Barnes Foundation, Merion, Pennsylvania, USA/Bridgeman Art Library. *Woman Hanging up the Washing* (1887) by Camille Pissarro, Musée d'Orsay, Paris, France/Bridgeman Art Library/Giraudon. *Portrait of Felix Feneon in 1890, Against a Background Rhythmic with Beats and Angles, Tones and Colours* (1890) by Paul Signac © ADAGP, Paris and DACS, London 2004, Museum of Modern Art, New York, USA/Bridgeman Art Library.